Eeyore Finds
Friends

Disney's
Winnie the Pooh First Readers

A Winnie the Pooh First Reader

Eeyore Finds Friends

Adapted by Isabel Gaines

ILLUSTRATED BY Josie Yee

DISNEY PRESS

NEW YORK

Eeyore Finds Friends

One lovely spring morning,
Gopher popped out of a hole
right beside Eeyore.

7

"Say, sonny," said Gopher,

"why are you alone?

Don't you know

today is *Twos*-day?

You should be with a friend.

One friend plus one friend

equals *Twos*-day."

"I see," said Eeyore sadly.

Then he perked up.

"Aren't you my friend, Gopher?"

"Of course I am," replied Gopher.
"But I promised to spend the day
with Rabbit. Good-bye, sonny,
and good luck!"

11

Eeyore thought he would try

his luck with Owl,

so he set off into the woods.

Everywhere Eeyore looked,

he saw animals in pairs.

He saw two chipmunks . . .

13

and two possums . . .

and two bluebirds.

Eeyore hoped that Owl

was not part of a pair.

But as Eeyore walked

up to Owl's house,

he saw that Owl had a guest.

Owl and Kanga were having

a tea party outside with an iced cake

and everything.

"I get it," Eeyore muttered.

"Tea for two on *Twos*-day.

How nice."

As Eeyore walked away,

he saw two butterflies

fluttering above a flower.

There were two worms

inching along the path.

And two strange creatures

bouncing in the meadow.

Eeyore noticed that the creatures
were Tigger and Roo.

"I'm no good at bouncing, anyway,"
Eeyore told himself,
watching from behind a tree.

As Eeyore turned away,
he remembered that he had
only two more friends to see.

"Pooh and Piglet are probably
spending *Twos*-day together,"
Eeyore mumbled. "But who knows?
Maybe I'll get lucky."

But as Eeyore suspected,

Piglet was not at home.

Piglet was at Pooh's house.

Eeyore watched the pair

through the window.

"Oh, well," Eeyore sighed.
"I might as well go home
and sleep until *Winds*-day."

Just then Pooh saw Eeyore,

and hurried to the door.

"Hello, Eeyore," Pooh called.

"Would you like

to join us for a snack?

We're having my favorite—honey."

"But that would ruin *Twos*-day,"

said Eeyore.

"Today is *Twos*-day?" asked Pooh.

"I forgot."

Pooh scratched his head and thought.
Finally he said, "*Twos*-day
could *stay* forgotten!

We could call today *Fun*-day, instead.

It rhymes with Monday."

"I see," said Eeyore, though he didn't.

33

Eeyore followed Pooh inside
and the three friends had a *Fun*-day
which was three times as nice
as a *Twos*-day!

Can you match the words with the pictures?

bounce

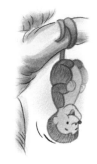

cake

Gopher

possum

worm

Fill in the missing letters.

chi_munks

O_l

hou_e

f_ower

wi_dow